4/09

DEMCO

Lost in the Mall

by Noel Gyro Potter
illustrated by Joseph Cannon

magic
wagon

visit us at www.abdopublishing.com

To my husband, best friend & partner—
For all of the countless children you have tried and will try to keep safe
including our sons, you are their hero and mine. oxoxox to infinity—NGP

Published by Magic Wagon, a division of the ABDO Publishing Group, 8000 West 78th Street, Edina, Minnesota 55439. Copyright © 2009 by Abdo Consulting Group, Inc. International copyrights reserved in all countries. All rights reserved. No part of this book may be reproduced in any form without written permission from the publisher.

Looking Glass Library™ is a trademark and logo of Magic Wagon.

Printed in the United States.

Written by Noel Gyro Potter
Illustrations by Joseph Cannon
Edited by Stephanie Hedlund and Rochelle Baltzer
Interior layout and design by Neil Klinepier
Cover design by Neil Klinepier

Library of Congress Cataloging-in-Publication Data
Potter, Noel Gyro.
  Lost in the mall / written by Noel Gyro Potter ; illustrated by Joseph Cannon.
    p. cm. -- (The adventures of Marshall & Art)
  ISBN 978-1-60270-198-4
  [1. Lost children--Fiction. 2. Brothers--Fiction.] I. Cannon, Joseph, 1958- ill. II. Title.
  PZ7.P8553Lo 2008
  [E]--dc22
                        2008003619

"Let's go, boys!" hollered Marti James from the family car. Marshall, Art, and Harley ran out of the house. They were excited for the trip to their favorite shopping mall.

3

When they reached the mall Art asked, "Can we check out Mort's Sport Court and meet up with you in a little while?"

"All right," Marti said. "But remember our side-by-side rule!"

"We know 'side by side with our eyes open wide!' We can take care of ourselves, right Marshall?" said Art.

"We're black belts, remember?" Marshall added.

"Black belts or not, strangers can take anyone by surprise," Marti said. "Stay together or no deal! We'll meet right here in 30 minutes."

"You're the coolest mom, ever!" yelled Art as the boys walked toward the sporting goods store.

Sport Court

Marti and Harley headed to a children's clothing store to get Harley a new pair of dress shoes.

"Why do I have to get some goofy dress shoes for Uncle Rob's wedding? What's wrong with my school shoes?" Harley asked.

"Well, muddy sneakers really aren't in fashion for a wedding, Harley. Maybe they will be by the time you get married!" Marti joked.

Clothes From Your Toes to Your Nose

Actually, Harley didn't mind going to this store. Inside, there was a funny clown with crazy rainbow-colored hair who handed out balloons. The store even had a great big treasure chest kids got to pick a prize out of as they checked out.

Marti and Harley went straight to the shoe section.

"What about these, Harley?" Marti asked, holding up a pair of black loafers with shiny silver buckles.

"I like these, Mom!" shouted Harley over the noise of the store. Marti looked at the shoes Harley had chosen. She smiled and shook her head no. Then, they both kept looking.

Once they found a pair of dress shoes that they both liked, they were ready to go. Marti paid and took the bag with Harley's new shoes inside.

Harley was carrying his treasures, too. He had a bright red balloon and a shiny blue balloon in one hand. His prizes from the treasure chest were in the other.

"We'll be right on time to meet Marshall and Art," Marti said. She hurried Harley out the door.

As they walked through the mall, Marti couldn't help but gaze into the beautifully decorated windows. Harley was having a great time watching his balloons bounce into the shoppers.

"There's Marshall and Art, Harley. Let's get out of here. The mall is getting so crowded!" Marti said.

Art spotted their mom first. "Hey, Mom!" he said. "We saw these awesome skateboard ramps. Can we show you? Dad would love them, too! C'mon!"

"I really want to get home, boys. We'll come back some other time with Dad. You can show him the ramps then, okay?" Marti said.

"Mom, where's Harley?" Marshall asked nervously.

"He's right here . . . ," Marti said. But when she looked down, Harley wasn't there!

"Wait, he was just standing right next to me holding his balloons!" gasped Marti. She began to shout, "Harley, Harley!" There was no sign of Harley or his balloons in the crowd.

"Marshall, Art, do you see him?" Marti shouted, giving away how very upset and frightened she was. She began to look around frantically, trying to search everywhere at once!

"Mom, he won't answer unless he hears the secret word," said Marshall.

"What secret word? Marshall, this is no time for games! We need to act fast! I'm going to the security booth. You two wait right here," ordered Marti. Then, she bolted off for help.

22

As she rushed off, Marshall and Art each began to yell "Rocket" loud enough to be heard over the bustling crowd.

From behind a huge planter, Harley heard the secret word. He ran toward Marshall and Art as fast as his little legs could carry him! He leaped into Marshall's arms!

Marshall and Art hollered to their mom, "We have Harley! He's okay!"

Near tears, Marti came running back to the boys. She hugged Harley hard. Then she asked, "Harley, where were you?"

"I dropped my prizes," Harley explained. "When I picked them up, all I saw were legs and feet. You weren't next to me anymore. I got really scared, so I hid behind the planter where no one could see me. I didn't want strangers to know that I was lost!"

"I'm so sorry, Harley. I should have been watching you! I broke our side-by-side rule. Thank goodness you saw your brothers!" declared Marti.

Harley sprang back and said, "I didn't see Marshall and Art, Mom. I heard the secret word!"

"What secret word?" Marti asked.

Marshall explained, "Mom, you must have been so scared you forgot. We said that if we ever got lost or if someone else was picking us up from school, we should only go with someone who knew our family's secret word. Harley chose Rocket because our dog makes him so happy."

"Thank goodness it worked! Marshall, Art, I am so proud of both of you. You used your heads and you didn't panic. Let's go home now. It's been quite a day," sighed their mom.

As the car pulled into their driveway, they could see their dad was already home from a day at the karate studio. Marti told Johnny all about losing Harley.

Johnny tried to comfort his wife. "It's okay now," he said. "We learned something from the boys today—have a plan and be prepared before something happens."

"They weren't scared, they were aware. Just like we've taught them, Johnny!" said Marti.

"We were fortunate today. C'mon. Let's all go take Rocket—I mean our secret word—for a walk," suggested Johnny.

"Hey, Dad, I think Rocket would be proud to know that he's our secret word, don't you? I wish I could tell him," said Harley.

"Well, Harley," Johnny chuckled, "if you do tell him, one thing is for sure. He'll definitely be able to keep our secret word a secret!"

Lost in the Crowd Tricks

Crowds create great opportunities for strangers to look for victims. It only takes a moment to be startled by a stranger, enabling them to carry or lead a child away out of view. You can and should be prepared! Here are some valuable and important stranger danger tips:

Children:
- Stay close to a parent, teacher, or guardian, especially in crowded places! Don't wander off or permit a stranger to speak to or approach you! If they do, point the stranger out to those you are with.
- Make a plan for situations, such as getting lost, *before* they happen. When you arrive anywhere, have everyone agree on a special place to meet if you become separated.
- If you forget or can't find the special place, stay calm. Find the nearest police officer, security guard, or worker wearing a badge or uniform, they will help and protect you.
- If you can't find a store employee, go to a family with several children for help. The parents of that family can help you find your parents or guardian!

Adults:
- Remind children where you are to meet every time you arrive at your destination, even when visiting regular neighborhood locations.
- Teach children to firmly shoot up their arms and keep them straight in the air above their head with their fingertips touching. This technique prevents anyone from being able to pick a child up under their arms!
- Without instilling fear, make children aware that a stranger is *anyone* they do not know; male or female, teenager or adult. *Caution is key* and a great preventive measure!